COMMON THREADS
ADAM'S DAY at the MARKET

NOTE TO READERS

Over time, we all may find that we've been taught to favor certain appearances or cultural norms over others. But we know that children (and adults!) are most successful when they are able to collaborate and thrive with people from all kinds of backgrounds. Diverse collaborations lead to increased empathy, understanding, innovation, commitment to social justice—and more! This story is one that facilitates conversations about diversity and encourages readers to recognize diversity as an advantage in their communities.

By HUDA ESSA • Illustrated by MERCÈ TOUS

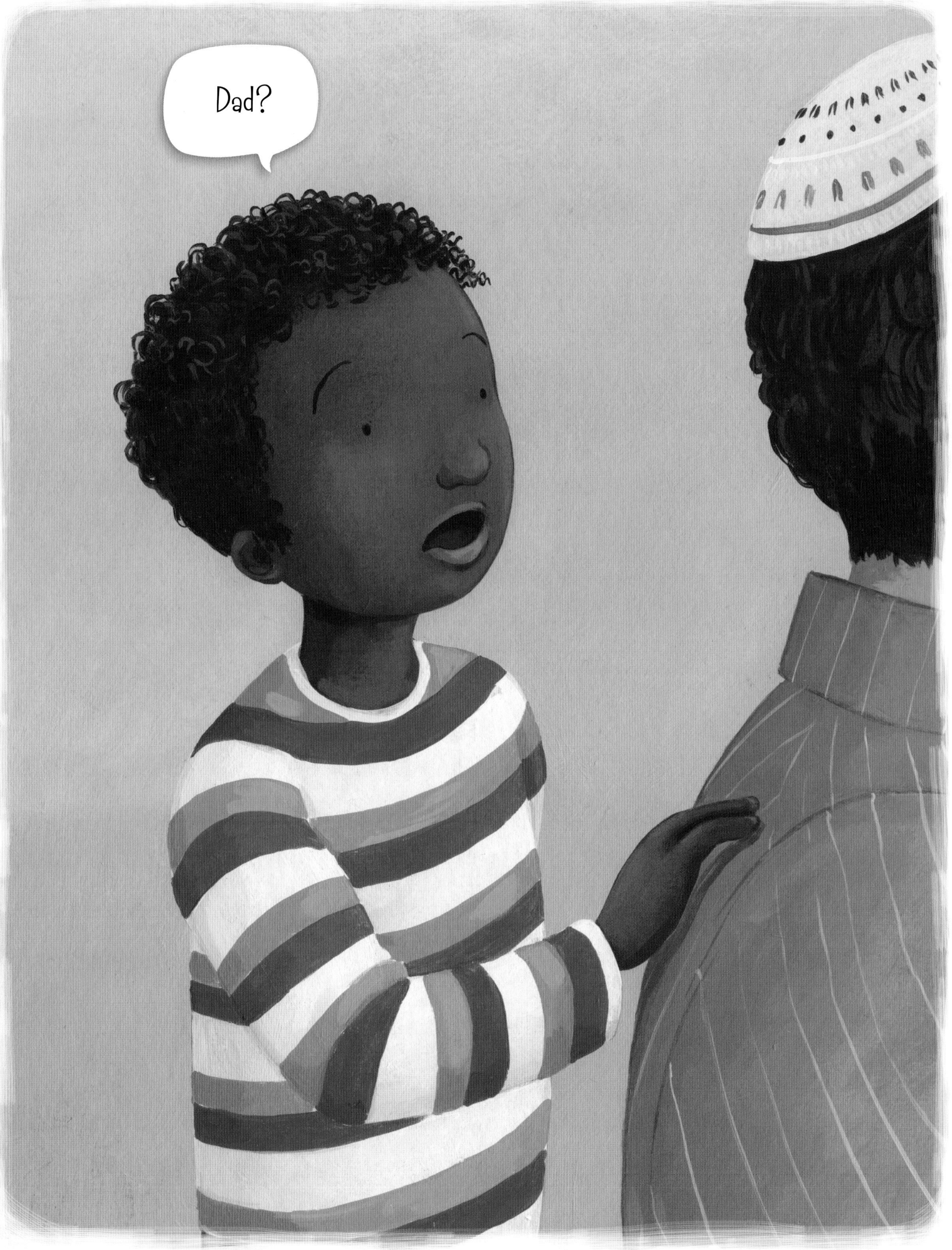
Dad?